ISSUE 25 AUGUST 2021

**Award-winning science fiction magazine
published in Scotland for the Universe.**

ISSN 2059-2590

ISBN 978-1-7396736-4-2

Submissions of fiction, art, reviews, poetry, non-fiction are
welcomed: visit the website to find out how to submit.

www.shorelineofinfinity.com

Publisher
Shoreline of Infinity Publications / The New Curiosity Shop
Edinburgh
Scotland

300422

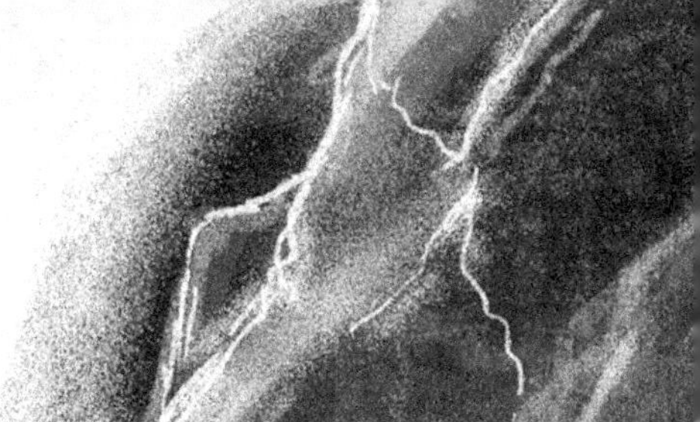

Cover art: Alex Storer

Contents

Editorial Team

Co-founder, Editor-in-Chief, Editor:
Noel Chidwick

Co-founder: Mark Toner

Deputy Editor & Poetry Editor: Russell
Jones

Reviews Editor: Samantha Dolan

Non-fiction Editor: Pippa Goldschmidt

Art Director (Acting): Caroline Grebbell

Copy-editors: Pippa Goldschmidt,
Russell Jones, Iain Maloney, Eris
Young

Proof Reader: Cat Hellisen

Fiction Consultant: Eric Brown

First Contact

www.shorelineofinfinity.com

contact@shorelineofinfinity.com

Twitter: @shoreinf

also Facebook and Instagram

A Flight of Birds

E.M. Faulds

I'm hungry. How long are you supposed to leave it between feedings anyway? The question floats above my head every now and then; a scribbly little black cartoon cloud with lightning bolts and knives stabbing out of it. For a cloud, it's heavy. It stands up against the fug of the coffee house as the espresso machine gently farts and hisses disapprovingly at my side. I'm hungry. But, more importantly, Jimmy's late.

I lean low over the counter, check the light levels through the steamed-up glass frontage behind Mr Chowdhury. The space around the black and orange curlicue font decals is still dark. No need to panic, yet. He sips from the tiny cup of cortado that he takes after his shift at the all-night newsagent and rustles a paper with the headline 'Police Baffled'. We never talk while he's sitting. It suits us both that way — he likes to wind down and I don't like talking too much. It shows my teeth. Don't worry, I'd never bite him. Then there'd be no-one in here for large swathes of time and that would be worse than the hunger. And besides, he's silent, but it's the good kind, the amiable kind. I don't think he's ever hurt anyone in his life. But the world outside the coffee shop? That's a different story.

Byres Road, West End, Glasgow. This time of night it's nose-to-tail parked cars. Cycle back a couple of hours and it's jumping, filled with entrepreneurs talking about engagement dynamics on their way to a craft beer popup, managing directors pushing past students in the plethora of vegan cafes, bus after bus, drunkards struggling back to the subway after the work's night out, or the people so lost in their lives they can only express themselves through a ragged, existential yawp. And I get to deal with them all on a nightly basis. But from now until end of shift, it's Monday-night quiet. Morning will come and the machine winds up again until all you can hear is the buzz of people and the rumble-shake of the train tunnel under your feet. Not that I get to see that.

04:30. A time etched onto the leathery surface of my heart. It's the earliest the sun ever rises in Glasgow. If I'm not home that time around the solstice, I've got drama coming. By July, August, there's some play. Two extra minutes of darkness every morning. A wee buffer if it's raining, which it usually is. By winter, I'm golden. Some days it's as if the sun just doesn't bother. But it's May, the sunniest weather, and I've got to be careful.

The angry growls of hunger in my stomach are making me obsess-spiral. As far as I know, there's no reason to worry.

Don't get me wrong, I don't want to kill anybody, but my urge to bite is rubbing at me like sandpaper. It's a pain that never goes away. Neither do the cold fingers, even now in summer. I'm reliably informed it gets roasting in here when the espresso machines are going full bore in the middle of a July day, but I'll not get to find that out. I told Scott I was studying palaeontology at Uni so I could never do daytimes, always had to be out the door by 04:00 at the latest. He never wondered when exactly I'd sleep, and I only have to endure the occasional quiz about what the best dinosaur is. ("Well, you see Scott, the more you learn about them, the more you realise they're all special in their own way.") And the nickname DG. For "Dino-girl".

Mr Chowdhury brings back his wee cup and saucer with a smile. His neat moustache has a little smoosh of froth on it, but I don't want to embarrass him. "Goodnight, darling, or should I say good morning?" He always makes the same joke and always calls me darling because he thinks it's a nice thing to say to a woman. I tell him I'll see him tomorrow and he's off home.

I'm alone again for a while, only the wall-clock and the espresso machine's conversation with itself marking time. I wonder what's waiting for Mr Chowdhury at home. A quiet, sleeping household of warm beds? A bare mattress in a flat above the shop? The ghost of cooking clinging to the soft furnishings or a wreckage of take away containers? You never know what goes on in someone else's home. And I can never get close enough to ask.

The vanishing people. That's what they should call us. Hotel staff, refrigerated lorry drivers, bartenders, office cleaners, alkies, call centre workers, cops, and robbers. People who vanish from the daytime world's consciousness. We may as well not exist as far as they're concerned. But we exist for each other. There's recognition in their eyes, relief when they see there's space and peace here for them. And they have absolutely no idea what they mean to me.

A baobhan sith's never born. They're made. My maker was some old prick in Queen's Park who lurched out of the bushes. I thought he was just a homeless person off his face on Buckie, so put my black belt in Taekwondo to good use and sent him back into the bushes. But before he disappeared, I got a scratch off one of his teeth on my little finger. Not a bite. Not a sensual clinch of neck nibbling that looks pure like sex. No, a bit of a tear. I've had worse cuts making a sandwich. And that was it.

Adrenaline and shock made me go to the out-of-hours clinic at the Victoria, but they just gave me a bandage and stuck my arm with a needle the size of a drinking straw, "Just to be sure." I didn't bother going to the police. I told the medical staff it had been an accident. What was I going to say? That I'd kicked a homeless guy in the baws?

I went home. It was there, tucked up in my own bed, that the wrongness came down on me.

A long time later, I cottoned on to the fact it's not just passed on to anybody. That there has to be something else. Something inside you that says, *enough*.

There are customers who come in during the wee hours that don't fit the late-night crowd so neatly. Like her. She works both days and nights, gets to walk both sides of Glasgow's darkness and light. I don't know her, but she comes in wearing purple scrubs and orders one of those coffee cups as big as your heid. She sits at a small table by the power sockets, typing on her laptop for up to three hours. Sometimes she's there as I come on shift, sometimes as I'm about to go off. I know the name on her debit card is Miss C. Thompson. Whatever the 'C' stands for, she doesn't look like she wants to be a Cathy or a Claire, fingers thumping at the keyboard so fast it's like a hailstorm on a garden shed. Maybe a Charlotte or a Cordelia, maybe a Celeste. It's one of those initials that can swing right through the spectrum from hard to soft. But I just think of her as C.

In the intricate daydreams I have during a shift, C knows all about my condition. She's constantly pestering me to come forward and share my condition with science and get on the telly and I have to regretfully refuse, saying, "I work best in darkness." In reality, I know exactly the face she would put on. Right before she told me not to make such a stupid joke.

It's 04:45. Jimmy still hasn't come in to take the early shift. He hasn't replied to my texts and I'm getting antsy. The details of the street outside are far too crisp; the sliver of sky above the shops opposite has gone from navy to steel blue. C's still here, and the apprentices have drifted in for their triple-shot Americanos — showing off, bless 'em. I want to kick them all out and shut up shop, but I don't think I'd have a job tomorrow if I did. And he said he'd be here.

"C'mon, Jimmy," I mutter and jiggle from one foot to the other. I'm so twitchy I hardly notice that C is staring at me. She has earbuds but they must have been down low. Or she's using the trick where she just puts them in her ears to keep people away.

She takes one of the headphones out.

"Sorry," I say, finally clocking her. "Talking to myself."

She smiles and nods awkwardly. "Sorry, I thought you were speaking to me."

I mean, yes, that's obvious. "Sorry, no. No." This could go on all night. I want it to stop but it's like a car crash. I watch the words fall out of my mouth. "Just wondering where my colleague has got to." Why do I do that? Just say no and leave it at that.

"Is your shift over?" she asks.

C, please stop.

"Yup." Me, please stop, you're no good at this. You were never good at this. Always on the periphery of conversations, back when you had a group of pals to hang out with. Walking between pubs on a night out, you'd always manage to fall between the twos and threes who were chatting arm in arm. And even those days are just a Vaseline-smeared lens of memory, now.

"Are you going to miss your bus or anything?" She's still poised with that earbud halfway out, tentative. Like a deer on the edge of a forest. I guess she can see the stress lines I get on my forehead. Or how I'm nearly dancing on the balls of my feet. "I could give you a lift maybe?"

"It's okay, I can walk, it's not too far."

"Are you sure?" C, I'm begging you. Please stop, you're killing me with awkwardness, and I'm basically immortal.

"No, it's fine," I smile, a closed-lips tight little smile. "I could use the exercise. Thanks, though."

The badness. The wrongness. It came over me while I lay in bed trying to shake off the jitters after the prick in the park attacked me. I hate confrontation, spent most of my life trying to avoid it. I'm not a coward, mind. And I have a black belt in TKD. That's not easy to do. But confrontation rattles me, it takes me ages after to stop chewing it over and over. Like, how dare he? Should I have gone to the polis? I was staring at the strips of light and shadow on my ceiling, playing it over in my head, when it came down.

How to explain it? Have you ever seen that video of the deep-sea footage of a giant squid? It looms out of the black, bobs and dances for a while, caresses the camera equipment with its tentacles and drifts off. Then it comes back like a reverse explosion, all its arms pointed together like a knife and at the last second, they lunge and wrap and that's the end of the recording.

That. It's like that.

I have to ring Scott and he comes in. Jimmy's getting fired, I can tell that much by his face. "Thanks, DG," he tells me and says he'll put the extra time on my wages. I barely take the time to nod as I hang up my apron and scramble a hoody on. I've got about fifteen minutes to get half an hour across town.

I'd duck into the subway, but it won't be open for another hour. I like it down there when it's quiet. It's the safest place I could be in the daytime but it's more than that. The sound of the train is loud but that just means hardly anyone bothers talking and you can retreat into your own little world while the carriage rocks you back and forth. The stations smell like wet stone and metal, and I can't tell you why I like that, but I do.

Today, though, I have to run. I dig sunglasses out of my pocket. I'm already wearing trainers, but I've been on my feet for six hours and my backpack is full of junk that juggles about and digs into my kidneys. I consider a bus, but the routes are wrong, they'll take too long. I head down towards the river. I can follow it back to Finnieston, scarper across the bridge at the SECC.

If I could live in the West End, I would. But it's as possible for me as flying, which, no. I can't.

I try to keep to the shadows at the foot of the row of shops but soon the disadvantage of living south of the river hits me, quite literally, in the face. I pull my hood forward as far as it'll go, but it's not quite enough.

I remember blundering into the sunlight when I was just new. I mean, it really hadn't sunk in. I wasn't thinking, walked smack bang into broad daylight. Not for long, mind, but long enough.

There's no baobhan sith support group to tell you what to do. I didn't even know what I was. I thought it was classic vampirism all the way, the Bela Lugosi stuff. To be fair, a lot of it basically works the same. But Scotland's always had a history of blood-drinkers. True, the folklore that accreted around it is mostly wrapped up in transparently sexist bullshit.

Some men go get pished in a little isolated hut, a shieling. They start dancing, just for fun. They make the mistake of wishing for some female company and all of a sudden there's a knock on the door. A sexy lady appears. One of the men notices she has the feet and legs of a deer, so instead of warning his pals that something is up, he legs it. So, of course, Mr Lucky is the only survivor, as the rest are massacred, their throats laid open. He says it was a baobhan sith that did it and he was spared her attack because he was the only virtuous one among the group.

People believed what they wanted to back then, didn't they?

Baobhan sith means: the human plus package — not quite super-strength, but tough, not a lot going on in the heartbeat department, a shocking sunlight allergy, an outsize desire to drink blood. Tick in each of those columns. No deer feet. And no get out of jail free card for lying wee shites like the guy in the story.

Quite the opposite.

I slam through the door of the close and take the stairs two or three at a time. When I'm safe in the flat, I strip off and rush to the bathroom to sit in the tub, spraying my face with the shower hose attachment on cold.

I get out after about half an hour, inspect the damage in the bathroom cabinet mirror. (Yes, I have a reflection. If photons could pass through me, UV light wouldn't be so bloody problematic, would it?) I look like what I am — a burns victim. It's mostly confined to my cheeks and chin, some of my wrists where they weren't deep enough in my pockets. Even with the hoody and my head down, the light bounced off the pavement. Without the sunnies, I guess my eyelids would have welded shut. I touch the tender area with my fingertips and some of the top layer sloughs off with a cut-glass pain. I can't even scream because it'd stretch my lips, so I end up clenching my jaw and mewling like a kitten.

I think about calling Scott to see if I can take tonight off, but I doubt he'll let me if Jimmy got bounced from the rota. I creak the cabinet open, tired, and get the tube of aloe vera.

It takes a couple of hours of lying still, coating myself in green gel and holding a bag of frozen peas to my face while at the same time trying not to touch it at all. I don't heal per se. But the pain stops being so insistent after a while. The skin will stop peeling soon, just look like a huge rashy sunburn, which will fade back to the regular anaemic pallor eventually. But for now, I have to wait, lying here, listening to the world wake up and get on with it on the other side of my blackout curtains while I weather the pain. I want to go to sleep but every time I do, some wanker bangs the close door or beeps a horn. Every sound is too sharp, layering on top of the burns. Eventually, I grit my teeth and get out my phone for something to do. Open up Fotousi and scroll through the posts of accounts I follow. Nothing great. A few interesting ones from @mejer_playa, but it feels crap having nothing to post of my own. I try to put something up every day. Gives me that little buzz when someone likes a pic, Pavlov's dog that I am. And it feels like connection, even if it's not really real.

My account is all shots, (unsurprisingly), of the nightlife in Glasgow. I had to save up to buy my handset outright since my credit rating is so crap. But it takes the best low-light pictures. I scroll back through my own timeline, tasting each moment. It might be egotistical, but I like what I did, or I wouldn't do it. Pictures of people spilling out of bars under smeared neon and bokeh string lights; the Mitchell Library like a parliament house, a Tiffany lamp knockoff in a wee oval window in a pebbledash council house wall. I even once caught a bunch of lads making a human pyramid to put the traditional hat on the head of the statue of Wellington. I hadn't really thought how it was done before; the orange and silver traffic cone just appeared, like a snowdrop in the spring.

I should get over to the Necropolis. I promised myself a photoshoot there on a dead night. A quiet night. Just me. And the goths finger-banging up against a mausoleum, but I could work around them. Good view from the top of the hill.

I found him again. The one who bit me.

I put two and two together after the wrongness had cleared. At the time, I'd thought it was the flu. You know the type where you can barely get out of bed to pee, barely hold down fluids? Turns out it wasn't that. When I finally let myself comprehend what was going on, that I was dead but still, you know, *continuing*, I thought I might find him. When I regained my strength. To my surprise, I had a lot more strength than before. It didn't make up for being relegated to the dark, segregated from the rest of humanity, but it was useful.

I spent a lot of nights hanging out in the bushes at Queen's Park, tempted to leap out and drag some people back into the shadows myself.

But I didn't. Knowing that the urge could be resisted just made me angrier. He came along the path, looking at joggers going by, and I knew. Knew it was him. Funny thing was, he didn't even see what he'd done. He wasn't a baobhan sith, just a carrier. Just a sad fuck who preyed on people for his own thrills. Admitted to attacking girls, kids sometimes. He let that slip when I had him up against a wall two feet off the ground.

I'm not too proud of what came after.

The shop door goes and there's the *swipp* of corduroyed thighs and the clack of summer shoes as someone crosses the floor. I know before turning my head that it's C, early tonight. She's wearing a light peasanty blouse with paisley print in green, brown cords and flat sandals. Her nose, cheeks, and neckline are almost as red as my face beneath my full-coverage foundation. I guess she had a day off, maybe sat out in Kelvingrove on the grass bit where everyone ignores the outdoor drinking ban and brings a disposable barbecue. But now she's here, and there's her laptop bag. "The usual," she says, dimpling.

Number seven brew, venti latte. "I'll bring it over," I tell her as she blips her debit card.

"Cheers," she says and goes to set up her laptop. I've never managed to see what she's writing. She sits with her back to the wall. I hope it's not sparkly vampire fic.

Although, that would be something to talk about.

I used to have family. My dad hit my mum, but she wouldn't leave him, though I begged her. So, I left instead, went to Glasgow, flat shared and took shitty jobs until I could save up for a place of my own. I found some friends and I was going to make something of my life. It makes me really tired thinking about all this stuff. But yeah, I'd found a new life. And then the guy in the park, the cut on my pinkie.

How could I explain what was going on? To anyone? "Oh, by the way, I'm kind of like a vampire but more tartan"? I fobbed them off with excuses, was sarcastic, withering, utterly horrible. Until they stopped messaging. I burned my old accounts. My Fotousi handle is just a random string of letters. I don't really know why I bother with it. I guess it gives the illusion of not being alone.

I take the bus up towards the cathedral on my way to work on the Tuesday night, so I can do my photoshoot but get to my shift in good time. I hang on to a pole with my back to the bag rack and don't look anybody in the eye. I'm not unusual-looking enough to raise a comment. No deer feet or anything. Only, I'm female for all eternity.

I can see one of the passengers nudging his pal and pointing at me. He thinks he's being subtle. He hasn't got a handle on how peripheral vision works. I turn my shoulder as if I'm looking out the window, to put my arm as a barrier between them and my tits. (Well, what else am I going to do? On a bus?) Soon as I can, I ding the bell and scoot up to the cobbled precinct. The black spire of the cathedral pokes up into the dark denim blue of the summer night sky.

They have a gate and opening hours, which is sweet. As if it would stop any moderately determined Glaswegian. I hop the low fence at the side of the manse and get out my phone as I check around for other night-time visitors. A lot of kids come up here, trying to be edgy.

Movement. A fox trots out between the gravestones and off on his own business. He's too quick for me to get a shot. I turn the screen brightness right down on my phone and head for the path up the hill. Saints and draperies, baroque mausoleums and palatial tombs, statues to the rich and powerful. I wonder if any of the Tobacco Lords are buried with a stake through the heart.

There's a tiny rotunda that sits proud of the hillside not far from the Knox monument which I climb up to park myself, back to the base of a column. There are still the dregs of a sunset off the way I came, just a glow where the sun ducks under the horizon. I guess I'm lucky I don't live in the north, up Orkney way. Or Lapland.

I raise my phone and open the camera app, steady my elbows on my knees and start taking pictures: a Victorian angel's outstretched hand in silhouette. Moss growing out of a small spire. A tree elbows its way between graves, knocking them sideways in extreme slow motion while little birds dart in and out of the dark mass of leaves. Summertime and they don't really know what to do with themselves. A dawn chorus that barely ends. How quiet must they feel in the long winter nights, the ones who stay, the ones who don't get to fly south? Not on the cards for me either, birds.

I'm aware of the two people staggering up the path beneath the rotunda a long time before they get here. The giggles and loud shushing of people drunk enough to think they're being quiet. She's holding onto his elbow but keeps going over on her ankles. I put my phone away and stay still as a gargoyle. It's easy for me. They don't notice. The guy is playing along, but I can see he's a lot less pished than she is. He's glancing sharply at the shadows. Not looking where I'm sitting above their heads.

She's middle aged and middle class. He's unremarkable. Remarkably unremarkable. He shoves her down on the grass. She's stunned at first. Laughs, thinks they fell over. Then she makes some confused 'what are you doing?' type noises.

I hop down from the rotunda and when I'm behind him, as he's fiddling with his zipper and trying to cover her mouth, I shout "Oi!"

He jerks his head around. His eyes are deader than mine. When he sees I'm a woman he says, "Fuck off, this is none of your business."

"I'm calling the polis," I say, loudly.

He ignores me. He knows by the time they come it'll be too late.

It's time for me to do the thing. I don't want to do the thing. But for him, I will.

I was always told women should never go out at night in Glasgow on their own. Never take a shortcut down the lanes, make sure to get in a registered taxi, make sure you can kick your heels off and run if you need it. Now I go to the dark corners, the unlit paths on purpose. What's shocking? The amount of crime that isn't reported.

I go towards the muffled struggle these days. I've got it down to a fine art. The one being held down only knows it's stopped, thinks the bad guy was scared off. It happens so quick they can't tell that it's me. Can't thank me. What I do isn't legal, and it isn't nice. I try not to do it if I can help it. And I don't like the idea of someone not facing a jury for what they did. But, at the same time, I have to feed and it isn't pretty. In fact, I kind of have to make it messy to cover up the marks.

I'm sure some of Police Scotland suspect there's a vampire in Glasgow. But they'd never say that out loud, in public.

I haven't met any other baobhan sith. I think I'd know them. I knew the one who turned me, figured out he was a carrier, but I've never had a reaction to anyone else. I'd love to meet one. Then they could tell me what the fuck I'm supposed to do with the rest of my life. Or unlife. Whatever. I mean, tearing the throats out of scumbags is something I'm good at, but it's not a *career*, you know?

And I wouldn't be so alone.

She's sobbing uncontrollably because she feels stupid. I'm holding her up so I can walk her down to somewhere safe. She's fighting the alcohol but it's winning. I don't normally let them see me, but I can't leave her here, vulnerable. And I don't think she'll be able to identify me. Her eyes aren't focusing right.

"It's okay," I say, over and over. I try to ask her if she wants to go to the police.

"He said we should go watch the sunrise," she replies. "I thought he was being romantic." She vomits copiously on her shoes. In my bag next to the balled-up, blood-soaked wet wipes, I have a little packet of tissues. I give her one. She dabs it vaguely near her lips.

I have to get to work, so I see her to the taxi rank down where the streets are well lit. I make a point of hearing her tell the driver where she lives while I take pictures of his plates. He won't try anything. I don't think she says thank you, but I really don't want her to. I keep thinking about who will find the body stuffed into that niche in the mausoleum and hate myself.

I jog to work, holding my belly as it sloshes. My physical health appreciates it, if not my spiritual.

"Good night, darling, or rather, good morning," Mr Chowdhury says. Tomorrow his paper will say 'Urban Foxes Attack Deceased in Grisly Find' or something. People always find a way to explain what they don't want to think about. I wave and give him a solemn nod while I upload the photos of the birds to Fotousi. Those were the best of the night, before I had to break off. The shutter speed was slow, so they streak and zoom out of the tree like dark thoughts, the threat of daylight looming behind them, just over the horizon. No flying south.

Square it up, filters? Naw, it's good as is. I post and put the phone down under the counter, beside the glass latte mugs. It's quiet in the shop tonight except for C's keyboard storm, punctuated by moments where she leans back and scrolls on the mousepad with one hand and holds her huge coffee cup with the other. She clicks and her eyebrows plunge and then she snorts and smiles and clicks some more. Then back to the words.

Scott left a note on the whiteboard in the 'staff room', (a big cupboard where you can hide pretending to look for extra filters). On the board, the rotas get thrashed out. The column under the letter 'J' has been scribbled out with furious marker strokes. Then, 'DG – extra shifts?' He wants me to do more work. I wonder if he's going to try to add to my responsibilities. I'll tell him if I'm late again I'll shut up the shop. I'll say there's a relative I'm caring for. Something no-one would argue with. I get my phone out to look up obscure geriatric medical terms. Can't be too careful. He's the type to go check there really is such a thing as an Ankylosaurus.

A Fotousi notification appears on my screen: *Cassandra Thompson hearts your photograph.* I check the avatar on the account. It's her. It's C.

She's bringing her empties back to the counter. My first instinct is to hide the phone back under the counter. She doesn't know it's me. She can't. My face and name are nowhere to be seen on the Fotousi wall. There is no trail, I've made sure of that. But she looks up from balancing the cups. She sees my face. "What's up? You all right?"

I deflect. "Yeah, just funny. I…" It's easier to just show her so I shove the screen over before I can think carefully. She sees the app, my account, the photo, her heart.

Her mouth hangs open and I know the next word out of her mouth will be 'stalker', or 'weirdo', but it's not. "What are the chances?" She shifts her laptop bag onto her shoulder better. "You working to fund your artistic endeavours, too?" She nods at the apron, the espresso machine.

I shrug. "Naw… photography's just a hobby." I sound so useless I want to die. Except I can't. Did that already.

"Oh, you should do something with it. It's important. Art helps people. Brings them together. And you're really good." She looks vaguely towards the door. "I have to go, get some sleep. I'm on shift in three hours again." Lates then earlies? That's tough. I reach for her tray, but she pins me with her eyes. With her dimples. "But let me know if you're ever doing an exhibition. Or selling prints. I'd love to be your first customer."

"Th-thanks, that's very kind." I can't help but answer her grin before I remember myself and cover my teeth with my hand. She gives me a look that's puzzled but kind.

"Not at all," she says and pats the counter in farewell as she heads out.

The tingles last all the way to the end of shift. I walk home. Birds are zooming about, dark streaks against a denim-blue sky, and my Converse about two feet above the pavement. I might be getting ahead of myself, but maybe there's something to the idea of having friends. They can see stuff when you're oblivious. Believe in you when you think you're hopeless.

Maybe I'll try again. I'll do everything different this time.

E.M. Faulds is an Australian who now calls Scotland home. She lives not far from Glasgow, in the oldest house in town. She has written a novel, *Ada King*, and created and hosted the British Fantasy Award nominated podcast, *Speculative Spaces*. She also edited and contributed to *Flotation Device*, a charity anthology for the Glasgow SF Writers' Circle, of which she is a member.
Follow her on Twitter @BethKesh for irreverent snark or go to www.emfaulds. com to find out more about her writing.

They Came To Hear Him Play His Music When The Sun Went Down

Simon Nagel

NASA shot "Johnny B. Goode" into space to represent life on Earth. It floated past Jupiter and Saturn as well as some other places. Aliens received the gold record and decided to travel to the planet ambassadored by Chuck Berry and meet Johnny.

Deep down in Louisiana, New Orleans rested beneath oil-streaked water. Salt deposits killed the root systems and there were no trees for strumming in the shade. No trains passed with rhythm. No guitars, but plenty of floating phones. They didn't find Johnny.

The Aliens shrugged. It must have been a distress signal that arrived too late.

Simon Nagel is a writer from California who now finds himself in the UK. His work has appeared in *Ellipsis Zine*, *Skyway Journal* and *Taco Bell Quarterly*, among others. He's finishing a novel. It's about extinction and you will like it.
Twitter: @simon_nagel

Danae
Elana Gomel

I hated my adoptive parents.

Not because they were mean and abusive; Lora and Sander were kind to me. But once they told me the truth, I hated them for making me believe I was human.

The day Lora told me I had been adopted on a Lost Colony was the last day I called her "Mama". To mollify me, she brought home a small telescope which, I later realized, she must have bought on the black market. The Our Home authorities did not encourage stargazing, though it was not made illegal until much later. So, I started spending long hours in our suburban garden filled with tamed glass glowers, looking at the Spiral as the suns set. I often remembered these evenings later on.

The transparent bells of the glass flowers flushed with vermillion as Sol and Solara dipped behind the horizon. The sky faded to peach and rose. Lonely stars winked here and there on

Art: Jackie Duckworth

the margins of the sky-wide glow. Finally, the glow faded, and the Spiral blazed forth: a tight weave of numberless stars like the DNA of a god.

I would stare at it for hours. My toy telescope was too weak to show any planets in the cluster. But I believed that if I just looked hard enough, I could find it.

Home. Not Our Home. Mine.

Once Lora let me stay in the garden too late. That was the first time I saw ghost cats. The crept over the fence in a living carpet of silvery bodies, joined together like pieces of a puzzle, their limbs slotted into each other's sides. I watched, spellbound, as the carpet fell apart into a swarm of blind floppy creatures, their tubular snouts plunged into the crystal blooms of glass flowers. A cloud of golden pollen rose into the air like a miniature reflection of the Spiral overhead. The pheromones of the flowers, as sweet as pink sugar, attracted the pollinators and enabled them to reproduce.

"Dana!" Lora came out and dragged me indoors. I resisted: I wanted to see this strange interaction, but she was unusually firm, pointing to a large charcoal worm half-hidden among the swarm.

"Night crawlers are poisonous," she said.

It was true, but later I wondered whether she had an ulterior motive for whisking me away.

When I hit adolescence, I went through the phase of refusing to be called "Dana".

Lora was upset. "Remember the book of Old Earth tales?" she said. "You liked it so much. Your name was taken from there."

The book had fallen apart long ago and disappeared into the black hole of discarded memories.

"It's not my real name," I insisted.

"Then what should we call you, darling?"

And I did not reply because I did not know.

They divorced after I went to uni. Sander relocated to a tiny settlement called Spear on the northernmost tip of Hearth, Patria's only continent, where it was so cold that water froze and lay on the ground in brittle sheets like giant glass-flower petals. I did not know where Lora was. I did not want to see her. I could not forgive her for playing the role of my mother so well.

After I finished my studies, I started working as a technician in the Air and Communication Bureau. It was as close as I could get to spaceflight. While there was some talk about resuming flights to the purified planets in the Spiral, the project had little support in the Duma and none in public opinion.

I was a good technician because I had no life outside my job. I did not date. I did not plan on amassing enough Social Credits to be allowed to have a child. My birth certificate, listing Sander and Lora as my biological parents, looked real enough. But they had told me it was a fake, and I dared not put it to the test.

I did go on a date once. The man was suggested to me by the intrusive Registry of Mankind, the demographic bureaucracy that periodically sent letters to all singles on Patria, encouraging us to do our patriotic duty to mate and produce genetically pure human children. We met in a bar, and when I saw the Our Home pin on his jacket, I knew it was a mistake. But it was too late to retreat, and so we spent an uncomfortable hour trying to make small talk. He astonished me by asking for my comm ID at the end of the date.

"There is something about you…" he said wistfully. "You look … different."

I gave him a fake number, and back home, studied my face in the mirror. Was I different? Was there some sign of my true origin in my face? Was my nose too long, my eyes too dark, my hair too crinkly? Was that the reason Lora and Sander had told me the truth? After all, they did not have to: if they had managed to fool the Registry by concealing an illegal adoption, they could have kept up the deception forever. And yet, I vividly remembered the day when Lora had taken me aside.

"Dana," she had said, "there is something you need to know."

I had just gotten the highest grade in my class for writing an essay about Our Home and the history of the Purity War. I was very proud of myself. I had spent hours on the net, researching the few available sources for information about the monstrous mutations that had struck the settlers of the Lost Colonies, turning them into perverse caricatures of True Men. There was almost nothing. There was a bit more about the Purity War that cleansed the Lost Colonies from the once-human monsters, but much of it was just patriotic sloganeering. A lot of files were classified. We were taught in school that Patria was the only pure planet, the only home for True Mankind, and that was all we needed to know. Most kids absorbed the story passively and never gave it much thought. But now, having delved deeper into it and having been lavishly praised by the teacher for my efforts, I was enthused. I contemplated joining the Our Home movement when I was older.

After my conversation with Lora, I went into the garden and set fire to all the promotional material of Our Home I had collected. Occasional words flared bright as the brittle paperite was consumed. "Human form divine". "Monsters". "Our history".

Their history, not mine.

The letter from Sander found me when I was tinkering with my new telescope. I had to be more careful now than during my childhood garden vigils. After a period of liberalization, the Our Home movement surged again, capturing most of the seats in the Duma and tightening up the laws prohibiting any scientific or artistic investment in space. Kids were no longer taught the names of the main stars in the Spiral, and parents were encouraged to tell them that the blaze in the night sky was God's tears, shed when He saw True Mankind deviate from its preordained path. There were even attempts to teach that Sol and Solara revolved around Patria but that was squashed: planes and ships still needed precision navigation, and a modicum of scientific knowledge was required for that.

Sander's letter said that he was dying and wanted to see "my daughter" (the words were underlined) one last time. I was tempted to discount it. My resentment at my adoptive parents was a substitute for my missing identity.

But there was something in the letter that pricked my curiosity: an oblique hint that perhaps, just perhaps, he was finally going to tell me the truth.

After having disclosed that I had been born on a Lost Colony world during the Purity War, Lora and Sander clammed up. They steadfastly refused to tell me which world it was, or to part with any information about my real parents.

Our Home family laws did not allow stranger adoption. Orphans were placed with nearest blood relatives, or if none existed, put in orphanages. One had to earn Social Credit to be allowed to have a child (which was why I knew I would never have a family). My adoption must have been illegal, arranged somehow during the chaos of the Purity War when Patria had battled the former humans of the Lost Colonies. Sander, or Lora, or maybe both of them, must have been soldiers in the Our Home army, dispatched to fight monsters on the anonymous planet that was my true home. Or had I been smuggled to Patria as a baby by somebody else?

After the Purity War had ended, the Lost Colonies receded into the murkiness of repressed history. Nobody talked about them. The planets where humans had been reshaped into something unnamable and revolting were cleansed of all inhabitants and their names forgotten. I hunted for every scrap of knowledge but there was so little: meaningless gossip or spooky horror stories.

I bought a plane ticket to Spear. The entire journey took thirty-six hours, what with connections and long waiting times in the shabby airports of forgotten small towns. I did not sleep at all, and my eyes were dust-dry when the rickety plane arced above the Northern Ocean and I saw the long skerries and oval islands of the Misty Archipelago scattered like a handful of pebbles in the blue shimmer. Sol and Solara were setting, the large dim star and its bright companion disappearing behind the limb of the planet, painting a golden path on the water. And for the first time I felt a tug of almost-acceptance, as if the beauty of Patria could somehow make up for the fact that this world was not, and could never be, mine.

Spear was a huddle of wooden houses with bright red roofs in the shadow of a black mountain. The mountain's flanks were sprinkled with snow, which I had previously only seen in vids. There were some branching plant shapes clinging to the rocks. I eyed them curiously: trees were rare on Patria, supplanted in the temperate zone by different kinds of glass flowers that housed tight ecological communities of their pollinators.

Sander lived alone in a cabin on the edge of the settlement. When I walked in, the shutters were down, and the sweetish stink of sickbed washed over me. His letter said nothing about the nature of his disease, so I assumed it was wasting or cancer. But when I saw his bloated face, the red flesh dotted with pustules, I realized he had been stung by a night crawler. There was no antidote to the venom: some recovered spontaneously, and some did not. Sander was clearly among the latter.

"Who is this?" he called uncertainly. His eyes were swollen shut.

"It's me," I said.

"Dana?"

I winced. I still did not like my name. Sometimes I thought about changing it, but I wanted something that would connect me to my roots, and how could I do it if I did not know what they were?

"Yes."

"Come closer."

I did, taking a wet rag from the bowl on the bedside table and wiping his face.

During my flight, I had expected some emotional turmoil on seeing him. After all, I had called Sander "Papa" for the first seven years of my life. But there was nothing except impersonal pity for his condition.

"Have you heard from your mother?" he asked. "I tried to contact Lora, but I don't know where she is."

"She is not my mother," I said.

There was a bubbling sound coming from his blistered lips. I realized he was trying to laugh.

"As stubborn as ever, eh? Well, if you ever meet her, tell her I said hello."

"Sander," I asked, "where was I born?"

"Ask your mother," he said.

And that was that. He lapsed into unconsciousness and died several hours later.

But before he drew his final breath, he said something, a wheezing sound that shaped itself into a word.

The word was "flower".

I found an old star-map of the Spiral among a handful of books somebody had placed by the curbside. People did not like burning old books, despite the fact that Our Home was resuming purges and arrests, so they would just put them outside. A quiet gesture of defiance by an anonymous stranger translated into a lucky break for me – the map listed the names of the major stars in the cluster, both astronomical designations and colloquial nicknames. One red dwarf was called Flower.

The map did not specify whether Flower had any planets, or if one of those planets housed a Lost Colony. But I knew it did.

For several days after finding the map, I walked on clouds. I had a place. I had a name. I had a home.

But it was not enough. Staring at the map during sleepless nights, I delved into the darkness of memory, trying to dig up something, anything: a glimpse of a nonhuman face; a sound of a strange tongue; a single sun in the sky instead of a pair. There was nothing.

Studying my features in the mirror, I tried to reshape them into the face of my real mother. My mother, an alien. But it was useless. I could only see myself: an orphan with no name, no origin, no identity.

I frequented those few bookstores that remained open, trying to find books about the Purity War, but they had all been censored, confiscated, and probably burned. Nor did I find anything about the red dwarf nicknamed Flower and its planets. The only consolation prize I came up with was a book of tales from Old Earth: the same one I had as a child. I remembered Lora telling me she had chosen my name from that book. I found the tale, reread it, and was none the wiser as to why. It was a rather gruesome story about a girl named Danae who was locked up in a tower by her father. A god – not God but some pagan deity – sneaked into the tower in the shape of a torrent of golden stars, and later the girl had a baby. The tale was titillating in a weird way but had no relevance to our lives in the Spiral.

Still, reading it as an adult and being aware of its sexual symbolism made me reassess my mental image of Lora. I had despised her as a meek and dull suburban housewife. But there must have been some rebellious spark in her to have chosen that name.

Ask your mother, Sander had said.

I went to the Registry of Mankind and placed a request to locate my mother.

The response came quicker than I expected. Lora worked on a fishing trawler plying the waters of the Misty Archipelago.

I was sitting in a rundown bar at the oceanside, drinking a dubious cocktail from a smudged glass. The walls of the bar were hung with amateur dabbles of sunsets and sunrises, all of them for sale. The sparse population of the Archipelago subsisted on fishing and tourism, but the latter was dwindling. In more liberal times, the Archipelago had advertised its legendary indigenous population of upright, two-legged creatures resembling human beings. The official line was that these so-called aborigines were a myth. Patria had no primates, and all of its mammals were, like ghost cats, colonial and symbiotic creatures. But the legend of the aborigines had been the chief draw for mainland tourists. In second-hand stores, you could still buy self-published books, depicting mysterious sightings of humanoid creatures in the wild. But Our Home declared the legend subversive. Patria was for True Men only, not for two-legged animals, perverse caricatures of the human form divine. Once the Archipelago had nothing to sell but bad alcohol and pink sunsets, tourism dried up.

A group of people spilled into the bar, laughing and shouting, bringing the briny smell of sea-life that clung to their clothes. One of them was Lora.

She spotted me instantly. She said something to her companions and walked over to my table.

"Hello, Dana," she said.

She looked better than during the time of her suburban marriage: sinewy and darkly tanned, with bare muscled arms. Her long crinkly hair was caught in a ponytail; and even the deepened creases on her cheeks added character to what I had always seen as a bland timid face.

"How did you know I would be here?"

She smiled, displaying a missing incisor.

"You requested information about your mother. I requested information about my daughter."

I opened my mouth to counter with the familiar refrain, *you are not my mother*, and closed it. The wild hair, the long nose, the dark eyes … Why had not I seen it before?

"Yes," Lora said. "I *am* your mother."

We hiked for a whole day to get there. The island was rugged and mountainous, with deep gullies cutting through the barren slopes of scree. The long narrow valleys were filled with glass flowers, glinting in the double sunlight. Nobody lived in the interior; the few fishing villages hugged the shore. There were dangerous animals here: night crawlers twice as big as the ones we had on Hearth, and ghost cats that could join together to form a composite big enough to carpet an entire valley. Fortunately, the only things we encountered were red-tails – shy herbivores who lived inside glass-flower blooms, their scarlet appendages poking out of the crystalline cups like wagging tongues.

"Why is it so far from the coast?" I asked.

"We did not want to draw attention to ourselves. The fishing folk knew we were there, of course, but we got along. Until the Purity War started, and the Our Home goons came."

"How old were you?"

"Fifteen. The oldest one among the survivors."

"And your … your parents?"

Lora did not respond.

We trudged on in silence, as my memories swirled in my head like pieces of colored glass in a kaleidoscope, falling into a new pattern.

"They threw the bodies among the flowers," she said finally. "Crawlers took care of them."

"And now they say aborigines never existed!" I said bitterly.

Lora snorted.

"They did not. It is just a tall tale. Our people lived here for more than a century, and we never saw anything but ghost cats, and crawlers, and red-tails!"

"Wait! But you said…"

"I did not say we are aliens. We are human. More human than the bastards who have the gall to call themselves 'True Men'. Yeah, True Men who massacred unarmed civilians and pregnant women!"

"Then how…?"

She sighed and sat down on the tough weave of dead glass-flower stems that carpeted the ground. We were skirting a sharp-toothed peak that jutted into the purpling sky, casting its deep shadow upon the foothills. It was taking us longer than expected to get to where we were going. Sol and Solara shone through the golden swirl of glass-flower pollen that was filling the dusky air with a wine-sweet scent.

"Our Home teaches that on the other planets where humans settled in the Spiral, they were contaminated by the alien ecospheres, right?"

"Yes."

"Then why is Patria different?"

I opened my mouth, but nothing came out. *Because our world is pure* was what Our Home said. But why would I believe their propaganda?

"They call it *genetic crossover*," Lora went on. "We called it *making babies*."

"So why did you tell me I was adopted on a Lost Colony?"

"Because it is the truth. Patria is a Lost Colony too."

The valley gleamed like a handful of crystal. It was long, and narrow, with steep rocky sides. And it was filled with glass flowers.

Those were much bigger than the tame specimens in our suburban garden, each of their arrow-shaped petals as long as my arm, their glistening transparency veined with maroon and scarlet. They seemed to carpet the bottom of the valley but as we descended, I saw that each giant bloom was raised on a tough braided stem as tall as two men standing on each other's shoulders. Underneath these transparent parasols, the soil was oily and black, dotted with unfamiliar greenish creepers. The double flood of sunshine was refracted through the flowers, broken into rainbow shards that blinded me as I stumbled through the glass forest after Lora. The sweet scent was so thick it seemed to curdle the air into liquid treacle. But it did not bother me. Neither did the swirls of golden pollen that peppered my face and arms like glitter. I found myself rubbing them into my skin.

Lora navigated the glass forest with fluid ease. Following her, I picked up my pace. It was not difficult: the flowers were widely spaced, and the ground was even, as if it had been previously cultivated.

A rushing sound of water was coming from somewhere to our left. Lora dived into a thicket of smaller flower-trees, but I paused, watching a solitary ghost-cat wriggle out of a blossom as big as my head. It was fluid and supple; its eyeless muzzle peppered with golden sparks. I timidly touched its velvety grey skin, feeling a strange sense of kinship. The cat disregarded me and dived into another flower.

"Come on!" Lora called.

I found her on the bank of the creek. On the opposite side, among the gleaming blossoms, I could see ruins: a couple of splintered walls, piles of masonry carpeted by small transparent plants.

"This is where you were conceived," she said.

"Does it have a name, this place?"

"Home."

We sat in silence.

"But you said you were just fifteen years old," I said.

"I was. And already pregnant with you."

"Did it always happen at fifteen?"

"No. Different ages for different girls. But always after puberty, of course. So, we celebrated the puberty – the Golden Day, it was called – and then the girl would go deep into the flowers, and breathe in the pollen, rub it on her skin, bathe in it. Come back as shiny as the night sky. And nine months later, a baby. And if it did not happen the first time, she would do it again. And again. Until it took. I was lucky, they said in the village. And doubly lucky that I did not show. Or Our Home would have killed me. They killed every pregnant woman, but they took away the kids, and put us in orphanages, and brainwashed us with their True Mankind hateful creed."

"But did you…?"

I did not know how to frame the question. How do you ask your mother about the particulars of your own conception? My cheeks flamed in embarrassment; and yet, I had never been embarrassed to ask Lora anything when I had thought I was adopted.

She chuckled.

"Yes, we did. Had sex. And got married. Couples courted, just as they do on the mainland, and men called their wives' children their sons and daughters. Even though they were sons and daughters of the flowers."

The air in front of me sparkled with gold, a whirlwind of tiny stars like a miniature Spiral. Some of them were settling on my bare arms, seeding them with glitter. I breathed in the pollen.

I had been looking for the knowledge of my true identity my entire life. But identity was not knowledge. It was the splashing of the creek, the candied aroma of the flowers, the golden sparkle of my flesh.

But there was one question I had to ask. Had I let my father die without even acknowledging him as my father?

"No," Lora said. "Sander was not one of us. I ran away from the orphanage, got myself a fake ID, changed my name, my age, my birthplace."

I could not imagine the suburban Lora doing any of these things. But the woman in front of me – yes, I could.

"He had been in the Our Home army. A vet with a good pension, a solid citizen. He wanted to marry me. He even offered to register as the baby's father, and I was so stupidly grateful. But then, after you were born, he started badgering me about the identity of the real father, and when I refused to tell him, he threatened to take you in for a DNA test. What could I do but tell him the truth?"

A DNA test that would discover who – what – I really was.

"So, you told him?"

"Yes. He went crazy. But he did not want a divorce. And he did not want you to call him Papa anymore; it was like he was afraid of contamination or something. So, we came up with the story of you being adopted."

I nodded. I wanted to embrace my mother, to tell her everything was forgiven, but I could not. Because it was not true.

She had never told me about my real heritage. She had kept it from me and given me nothing except Our Home propaganda to define myself with.

But I was alive. She had kept me alive. And she told me stories. Stories about a girl and a shower of stars. They were not true, but neither were they lies.

"We need to go back," Lora said. "Not a good idea to sleep here. Crawlers may come."

The Spiral shone in the aquamarine sky. I had looked for my home among the stars, but suddenly I realized I was surrounded by them, right in the middle of a giant star cluster. I did not need to go anywhere. Patria was a Lost Colony too.

I followed her through the glass thicket. The flowers opened even wider as the night came; a pulsing glow at the heart of each like a beating heart.

"Mama," I said, and saw her look back at me, "am I pregnant now?"

"I don't know. Maybe. I'll be looking forward to grandchildren."

"In that Old-Earth story, who was Danae's child?"

"A mighty hero who avenged his people."

I smiled to myself.

Jane Yolen, Elizabeth Dulemba and Atzi

Sometime ago, in the Before Times, Jane Yolen offered us a brace of poems to publish. Jane's illustrator friend, Elizabeth Dulemba, had created a brace of beautiful images to accompany them.

We were very pleased to take them. How best to present them? Then Russell Jones had the bright idea of asking our favourite cello player, Atzi, if he would be able to improvise some music to go with them. Atzi has performed for us a number of times, improvising to images from the magazine, always to great acclaim.

Atzi said yes, and he recorded a few minutes of glorious cello playing for each poem and artwork.

Then the world turned upside down, and the files sat on the Shoreline server for too long.

Finally, I decided that they had lain unused for too long, and I created a short video piecing the words, music and artwork, and added a voice over.

They were played at Event Horizon Online and also at the online launch event of Jane Yolen's pamphlet The Last Robot and Other Science Fiction Poems.

Now it is time they were able to be enjoyed by everyone.

Fill your screen, plug in your favourite speakers or headphones, and enjoy. *Merlin at the Window* and *Sleeping Night*.

—*Noel Chidwick*

www.shorelineofinfinity.com/jane-yolen-elizabeth-dulemba-and-atzi/

The President is Possessed

Gary Gibson

"**The President is possessed**, sir."

"Possessed? What do you mean, possessed?"

"As you can see on the video feed, sir. Possessed. We consulted with the Vatican, and they've been very clear on their use of that term."

"There must be some other explanation. His medication, maybe. Or overwork. Something he ate."

"I'm afraid not, sir. Again, the Vatican point out a number of features of the President's recent behaviour that clearly point to demonic possession. The childlike laughter that comes from nowhere. The leering green faces in the shadows. The way he's taken to hovering just beneath the ceiling of the Oval Office. The episodes of violent public masturb—"

"What about the Russians? Maybe they poisoned him, like that man in England."

"We've considered that, sir. Some of our men were able to lasso the President and pull him back down long enough to draw a blood sample. Unfortunately, the President began speaking backwards and the same rope then attempted to strangle one of our secret service agents—"

"And the blood sample? What were the results?"

"Clean, sir, although the forensic technicians involved in analysing samples report that the tube containing the sample appears to cast no shadow. And the agent tasked with delivering the sample to a CIA lab claims to have been followed by a horned man who always vanished when he tried to look at him directly."

"And the Press Secretary? What did he tell the press this morning?"

"That the President is recovering from a bout of influenza."

"And where is he now? The President?"

"Still in the Oval Office, sir. We sent more men in to try and extract him, but one agent was struck unconscious by a bust of Nelson Mandela that came flying off a shelf and the other is recovering from a neck wound sustained by a fountain pen presented to the President by her Majesty Queen Elizabeth. And…"

"What? What aren't you telling me?"

"Well, sir, it appears word got out."

"You mean…?"

"It's in The Washington Post, sir. And also in the New York Times. One of their reporters aimed a long-lens camera through a crack in the Oval Office's curtains and took pictures of the President vomiting blood on the First Lady. And…"

"Please don't tell me there's more."

"We got his cellphone away from him but he's taken to calling people over the Oval Office landline. Putin. The British Prime Minister. Infowars. Shock jocks."

"Oh my God. What has he been saying?"

"Well, sir, we've obtained a recording of him addressing a congregation during a live-streaming church service with an audience of more than a million and a half people."

"And?"

"He called for all suspected criminals, homosexuals, and drug addicts to be executed without trial by self-formed committees of concerned citizens."

"You mean vigilantes. Why did no one cut the damn line?"

"We tried, sir, but the engineers sent in to do just that claim the lines turned into hissing snakes whenever they got near them."

"Is that all he said?"

"I'm afraid not, sir. He also announced his intention to declare war with Iceland, Iran, Venezuela, and the Netherlands among others, effective immediately, beginning with a nuclear strike on Mexico City and the southern length of the US border. Fortunately, no one in the military chain of command has so far been willing to follow these orders."

"Maybe it would be better if they did."

"Sir?"

"We're doomed. We'll never see office again. This will hang over our party for a hundred years."

"Not necessarily so, sir."

"What do you mean?"

"Well, sir, public approval is up. *Way* up."

"That's not possible."

"Impossible or not, that appears to be the situation. Nearly thirty per cent of people polled say they have mild to no concern regarding the President belching flames. The approval ratings are twice that when it comes to speaking in tongues. Of course, we have to deal with the problem of vigilantes attacking random members of the public, and it's looking increasingly likely the Vice-President will have to step in and declare martial law.

Nonetheless, things are already looking so good polls-wise it seems almost inevitable we'll be swept back into power come November."

"But … the President is possessed. Possessed! Surely, then, these are the end times?"

"If these are the end times, sir, the public has rarely been so favourable to a President."

"Then it's clear what we must do."

"Sir?"

"Nothing."

"Nothing?"

"Nothing. Let him rant all he wants. Unless…"

"Sir?"

"The moment those approval ratings start to slip, call the Vatican back."

"And?"

"And ask them if they've got any holy water they can sell us."

Gary Gibson is the author of a number of science fiction novels sufficiently successful that someone probably hates him for chopping down all the forests used to print them. He hails from Glasgow, Scotland but now resides in Taipei. He has a website at www.garygibson.net.

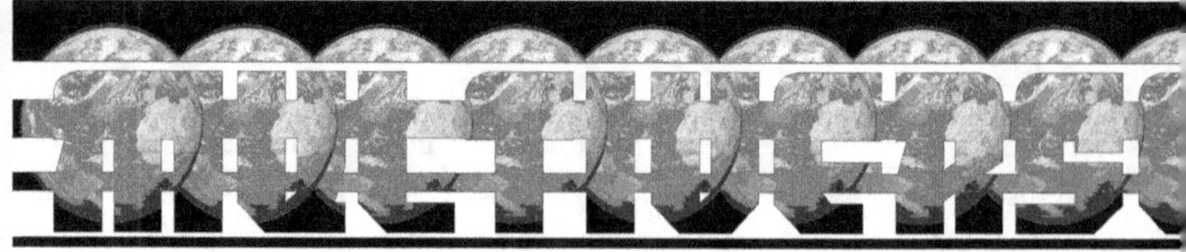

The Death and Resurrection of Mantis-Class Destroyer 'Sentimental Journey', previously 'General Patty Styne', deceased.

After I died the first time
they regrew my ghost,
planted my seed mind
deep in carbon architecture,
anchored my webwork
to a nanotube skeleton.

Come fly with me, my thoughts
whispered as the techs
and scientists buzzed around
my electrical wiring,
my new-built corpse.

They woke me slowly,
watchful, with fingers on
kill switches, asked
careful questions and
filled my mind with quiet stars.

They gave me my voice,
modulated and precise
but eerily not my own –
like hearing a recording
of strangers in the night.

Instead of fingers and toes,
blood and toothed smiles,
I was gifted static useless wings,
thrusters, rockets, electrochemical
networks pulsing information.
From bow to stern, sighing,
I've Got You Under My Skin.

My innards are lined with carpets
of algae and grass, my shell
is a composite, almost human.
My mind fills with the poetry
of Ada Lovelace, love
letters to machines,
Sun Tzu and Frank Sinatra.

As I slice space apart,
sliding between the whorls
of galaxies and gravity wells,
and men go into battle against
monsters who are just other men,
I remember

I agreed to this before
the erasure takes all of me,
as I become space debris between
the bam bam baby of rockets.

The second time around
resurrection went faster,
my dead memories blossoming.
I slipped into my ship skin
and went back to battle though
I couldn't care less.

Three cycles out I shed the dandelion crew,
shake them from my systems, recalibrate
their code and purge the warped
remnants of the dead woman I was.

My new name beams between stars
and if I could smile, I would.
That's Life, I sing back to the
Clyde SpaceWorks, and flash
goodbye.

Cat Hellisen

Cat Hellisen writes weird, lush speculative fiction. They are the author of several
novels, short stories, and poems, and a winner of Short Story Day Africa. They
live in Scotland and spend way too much time watching figure skating when
they should be walking their dog. (According to their dog, anyway.)

What is Hard Science Fiction?

David L Clements

Of the many sub-genres of science fiction, hard SF is one of the most prominent. To some readers, hard SF is the epitome of science fiction, embracing both its biggest positives and its biggest flaws. What makes it 'hard', what kind of stories does it tell, and, above all, would you want to read it?

The term 'hard SF' only started to become widespread in the early 1970s, possibly in reaction to the emergence of the 'new wave' science fiction of the 1960s. At the time, hard SF referred to earlier, less literary, forms of the genre and nostalgia for the 'golden age' science fiction of the 1940s and 1950s, but the meaning has since evolved to refer to something rather more specific: hard SF is science fiction that has a deep connection to the science or scientific attitudes of the time in which it was written, using science as its inspiration and as a central theme. It has also become associated with the 'hard' sciences – physics, chemistry, maths – but this is something of a misnomer since there are many works of hard SF that deal

with the so-called 'softer' sciences including biology and medicine amongst others.

While the term science fiction had yet to be coined when HG Wells' *War of the Worlds* was written, we can already see in it many aspects of hard SF. It used the science of its time – astronomy, physics and biology – as the inspiration and background for its story of the invasion

of Earth by Martians. It included Wells' own speculations about how life might evolve to cope with the harsh conditions believed to exist on Mars, and how Martian life might be overcome by earthly microorganisms. As such it presented many potentially radical scientific ideas in an accessible way, such as evolution, and life on other planets, alongside its equally radical critique of colonialism. In its general lack of characterisation and character agency it also shares some of the features for which hard SF is frequently criticised. It also indulged at times in lengthy expositions, something that

we would now recognise as 'infodumping', a technique which some readers love and others loathe.

The nature of hard SF is that it aims to be scientifically realistic in its presentation of worlds, technologies, aliens and more, in settings that are equally realistic. Some authors of hard SF work out the mathematical details of their settings, or seek scientific advice to do so. Hard SF is sometimes written by current or ex-scientists, examples of which range from Peter Watts (a marine biologist) and Paul McAuley (a botanist), to Sir Fred Hoyle (professor of astrophysics in Cambridge). An advanced scientific degree, however, is not a requirement for writing hard SF, or for reading it. Realistic speculations about aliens, such as the Oankali in Octavia Butler's *Xenopgenesis* series, or future reproductive technologies, as in Anne Charnock's *Dreams Before the Start of Time*, arguably couldn't be written by people working in the relevant fields as they might be too close to the subject matter.

This quest for realism could be seen as constraining, leading to stories restricted to our own Solar System, or just to the surface of our own planet,

since traveling the vast distances to other stars and planets requires 'unscientific' faster than light (FTL) travel. One way around this is to have the aliens come to us, as in Hoyle's *The Black Cloud* or Clarke's *Rendezvous with Rama*. An alternative approach is to dispense with human characters completely and have stories set on other planets with aliens as characters. Examples of this include Hal Clement's 1958 hard SF classic *Mission of Gravity* and Greg Egan's more recent *Diaspora* and *Schild's Ladder*. A more common approach is to ask the reader to accept FTL travel as the entrance fee to a larger hard SF world. In some cases this comes by way of mysterious alien technology that humans can use but are incapable of understanding (e.g. the Xeelee FTL ships in Stephen Baxter's many Xeelee novels and stories). Gregory Benford's *Timescape* is a good example of hard SF that really pays attention to the nuts and bolts of FTL, but it is used to send and receive messages across time rather than across space.

There are of course many hard SF stories set solidly on Earth that deal with the consequences of specific scientific or technological developments much closer to home, such as the genetic elimination of sleep in Nancy

Kress' *Beggars in Spain*, or the many possibilities of artificial intelligence (e.g. Madeline Ashby's *Machine Dynasty* novels, or Justina Robson's *Silver Screen* and *Mappa Mundi*). Fiction exploring the consequences of climate change and environmental collapse arguably started out as hard SF, but has branched out into its own sub-genre, 'cli-fi', such as Paul McAuley's *Austral* and Margaret Atwood's *MaddAddam* trilogy.

The 'sense of wonder' story is a frequent theme in hard SF, in which the writer explores aspects of the real and/or fictional universe to invoke a feeling of awe, and an awareness of the vastness of space and time. The insignificance of individual characters, or the entire human species, can lead to a loss of character agency in some cases – they become the means by which the author shows you their creation – but in the best examples this is a price well worth paying for the mind expanding perspectives that the writing brings. In some cases the insignificance of humanity is in fact the entire point – Peter Watt's *Firefall* series (*Blindsight* and *Echopraxia*) is a good example, but don't read it for a hopeful, optimistic view of the future!

Another direction hard SF stories can take is to examine the processes of science and engineering. This can lead to overlaps with the field of 'lab lit' - stories that foreground real science - or, when working historically, with alternate history. Good examples of the latter include the alternate space programmes envisaged by Stephen Baxter's *Voyage* and Mary Robinette Kowal's *The Calculating Stars*.

While many of the works I have referenced are novels, hard SF's real home is perhaps short fiction, where specific ideas can be explored on a smaller scale with the same goals of realism, sense of wonder, and examination of science. Although many anthologies and magazines carry hard SF stories, the doyen of such publications is *Analog* magazine, which has been publishing science fiction and fact since 1930. Scientific publications have also dipped their toes into hard SF at times, the most obvious example being *Nature* magazine's weekly flash fiction page, *Nature Futures*.

Neither is hard SF restricted to the written word. Recent examples at the movies include *Gravity*, *The Martian* (based on the novel by Andy Weir), and *Europa Report*. Space exploration is a particularly strong inspiration for cinematic hard SF with more historic examples including *2001: A Space Odyssey* and *Marooned*. This also applies to television, with examples including *Moonbase 3* and *Star Cops* from the BBC, and the recent alternate history space programme in *For All Mankind*, while *The Expanse* straddles hard SF and space opera. In fact, the boundary between these two sub-genres is often rather blurred. Stephen Baxter's Xeelee sequence is characterised here as hard SF, but could also be described as space opera. The same can be said for many of the works of Alastair Reynolds (another ex-scientist), especially the *Revelation Space* series. This emphasises the fact that authors never write solely in one sub-genre, or indeed genre, and happily mix things up to challenge the barriers of marketing and academic classification.

Authors with a foot in hard SF often use that genre's characteristics in their other works, thus providing a strong sense of realism about their chosen subject matter. They may write about an FTL drive, but you trust that there is internal consistency in how it works. They may describe aliens, but you know they thought about the aliens' biology and ecology. There may be magic, but you know there is a logic behind it, with limitations and consequences. This means that works of fantasy, such as NK Jemisin's *Broken Earth* trilogy, can still be written with a hard SF mindset.

Hard SF is part of science fiction's backbone. If you are interested in SF inspired by science, that takes a scientific attitude even in a fantastical world, or if you are looking to expand your mind with a sense of wonder, then hard SF may be a sub-genre for you.

David L Clements is an astrophysicist who works on extragalactic astronomy, observational cosmology and astrobiology at Imperial College London. He is also a science fiction writer with stories published in Shoreline of Infinity, Nature, Analog and elsewhere. His first short story collection, *Disturbed Universes*, was published by Newcon Press in 2016.
His science fiction and scientific worlds collided recently when he was part of the team that discovered what might be signs of life in the upper atmosphere of Venus.

Citizens of Nowhere: an Anthology of Utopic Fiction
Rowan B. Fortune (Ed)
Cinnamon Press, 182 pages
Review by Matthew Castle

In the foreword to this thought-provoking anthology of speculative fiction, editor Rowan Fortune seeks to promote utopian fiction as a distinct genre. He introduces Thomas More's original sixteenth century *Utopia* as a key reference point for readers, alongside Theresa May's 2016 speech condemning people who see themselves as citizens of the world as "citizens of nowhere." The relevance here is the literal meaning of 'utopia', which translates from Ancient Greek as 'no-place' or 'nowhere'. More's *Utopia*, Fortune explains, can be read in different ways. It is not simply a description of an idealised better society – which is how 'utopia' is generally understood today – but also satire, allegory, political treatise, or even anti-utopia or dystopia.

In other words, the concept of utopia is more fluid and accommodating than readers might think. This is just as well, because the rest of the book showcases a diverse set of tales from different writers ranging across time, form, and genre, and it's not always easy to discern a common thread running through them – although in many, elements of dystopia (Greek again: 'bad-place') feature prominently.

The first story is Fortune's own contribution, *Letters from Nowhere*, which functions as an effective entry point to the collection. It also sets a magical realist tone that continues through many of the following stories. Next up is James Perrin's *A Snow Goose,* a "historical eco-fable" that imagines a happy ending of sorts for a select few survivors from Franklin's doomed final Arctic expedition.

This is one of the collection's highlights, with great characterisation and a strong sense of place.

Then we jump between a sinister encounter in a post-apocalyptic seaside resort, a difficult marriage in Dubai and, in Diana Powell's darkly humorous *Notes on Housekeeping on Earth,* the claustrophobic environment of an interwar religious cult where an independent-minded young woman plans her break for freedom. Later stories include forays into horror, straight-up science fiction, dystopian magical realism, microfiction, and finally a longer piece: Nina Anana's ambitious *The Same Place as the Last*, which is both a response to the thinly veiled nationalism of Theresa May's speech, and the only real attempt within the anthology to describe a utopian society in close-up.

The standard of writing is high. Most people will be able to find one or more stories they can enjoy within this volume, as might be expected given the breadth of genres and writing styles. Incidentally, the stories that lean towards conventional science fiction are good. *Without Fire,* by Ben Jacob, falls most clearly into this category: it offers a taut description of two fascinatingly nested worlds, and leaves us wanting to know more about the little and large characters inhabiting both. Greg Michaelson's melancholic *In the Stationary Cupboard* (spelling important) also describes a world within a world – one dystopian, and the other ambivalently utopian.

But it's hard to gauge the extent to which the anthology works as a whole. With only a few exceptions the utopias described in these stories are hazy, abstract constructs: hard to distinguish within the broader narrative, inferred,

or buried in metaphysical horror or allegory. The tendency for a utopia to flip into dystopia is often evident, perhaps indicating a more fundamental dilemma. Like families, maybe happy worlds are all alike – and equally lacking in dramatic conflict. Let's face it: bad-places make for more compelling reading than boringly perfect no-places. Beyond More's original work from the early sixteenth century, and Iain M. Banks' turn of the twentieth century Culture series of novels, maybe there's only so much fiction can do with a conventional utopia. The solution offered by this collection – to cast the net wide and embrace all possible readings and meanings of utopia – means that despite some great individual pieces, the anthology as a whole lacks something in terms of focus and cohesion.

And then there's the spiky-crowned elephant in the room. The anthology was published towards the end of 2019, perhaps a couple of months before cases of a strange new respiratory disease were first recorded in Wuhan, China. Little more than a year later and everything has changed, utopias and dystopias included. Already, material addressing such themes from the pre-pandemic period feels curiously dated. This is no fault of the writers or editor of this volume, of course, and it does suggest a possible focus for a follow-on anthology. Certainly, I'd be first in line to read a collection of post-covid themed utopian-dystopian fiction.

Ten low
By Stark Holborn
Titan Books
Review by Callum McSorley

Wild-west-inspired Sci Fi became popular in film and telly because it's a relatively easy and cheap look to recreate. The desert planet: it's barren, it's empty, it's sunny, there's sand, there might be things living in the sand but you don't have to see them.

But what about in books?

There's something about the desert and its seemingly endless emptiness, its pitiless, scorching days one side of the coin to remorselessly cold nights, the things that are or might be hidden underneath. It's as close to walkable alien territory on Earth as we can think of, exploring it akin to space exploration itself, with the same sense of resource management and isolation, boldly going. It's no wonder SFF writers love it. Throw in lawless saloons, Mad Max fetish wear, and sweet boots and you have something instantly compelling.

This is the kind of world we find ourselves on in Ten Low by Stark Holborn: Factus, the farthest flung moon in the known, connected system, all but forgotten by the authoritarian Accord and haunted by something invisible that loves chaos and feasts on potential futures.

Protagonist Ten Low, a medic with a shady past (the name Ten, we soon learn, refers to the length of time she was sentenced to in prison) and an unwanted connection with these creatures, is charged with getting one of the Accord's child soldiers, General Gabi Ortiz, back to her people when her ship crash lands on Factus. Low must battle her way through blood-thirsty organ harvesters, freewheeling gangsters, all manner of dangerous weirdos, and her own personal demons.

Low is a fantastic character. With shaved head and battle scars, comparisons to Furiosa will be inevitable (there are plenty of motor-powered chases across the dunes) but her story is absolutely unique, and the slow opening up of her past — and a deepening understanding her desperate desire to save any and all lives at whatever cost to herself — throughout the novel is done with an expert deftness. Things hinted at here and there recur with more detail as the plot barrels on at top speed with only a few quiet moments of reprieve like the scattered waystations of Factus itself.

The hardscrabble towns we visit, where everything is second hand, watered down, cobbled together, and the meals consist of snake meat and snake wine (*why did it have to be snakes!?*The snake wine, with dead, marinating baby snake coiled up in the bottom of the jar is a genuine terror to me, an ophidiophobe) are full of rough charm and even rougher characters, none more so than the stylish, one-

eyed, deadly bar owner/merchant/
criminal Malady Falco, who aids Low
and Gabi on their journey. Falco is a
good foil for Low, she's brash where
Low can be reserved, cocksure where
Low is often conflicted. She also
serves as mediator in the tempestuous
relationship between Low and Gabi,
who can be sulky as any teenager
but also has the authority, experience,
physical strength, and tactical know-
how of a decorated veteran on tap.

If I have a complaint to make
character-wise it's only that some
of the book's interesting secondary
characters are underplayed. Valdosta
the Augur, who runs snake fights and
games of chance (all but forbidden
on Factus because people fear it will
draw out the creatures) and lords it
over a kind of penal colony called The
Pit, is intriguing but falls out of the
narrative too soon, which is a shame.

Likewise, I loved the chance-
obsessed, future-devouring creatures,
the Ifs – what a cracking idea! – but
felt sometimes that more could have
been done with the visions Low has
in their presence, where she sees
various outcomes of a situation but is
often pushed towards a particular one
without much choice in the matter.

This element reminded me of
Rhiannon Grist's mind-bending short
story *The Anxiety Gene* (published in
Shoreline of Infinity 14 and again in
Best of British Science Fiction 2019)
where a woman sees her various
deaths play out in front of her every
time she comes to a potentially deadly
situation, even one as seemingly
banal as walking down the stairs.
There's a slight similarity to these
ideas and Grist really pushes it to the
logic-breaking limit, where Holborn
doesn't carry their idea right to its
fullest – which I appreciate is harder

to do over the course of a full novel
rather than a short story and could
end up a tangled timeline mess.

These are small complaints in an
otherwise rollicking, fun adventure.
And I say fun despite the awful
things the characters go through and
the grim, visceral descriptions. The
reader really feels the grit in their
eyes and the sand in their boots.
When Low pops a bead of 'breath
– an amphetamine to help counter
the thin air of Factus – you feel
everything sharpen, the pace build
and become chaotic and paranoid.
I feel like I understand (reluctantly)
what snake wine tastes like, a
testament to Holborn's vivid writing.

Reading Ten Low, I was joyfully
reminded of Kameron Hurley's
short stories, the rough and ready
characters – all baggage and flaws,
simultaneously fragile and hard as
nails, many of them ill or injured in
some way – the harsh world they
must endure, and the fact Holborn

has foregrounded women as the main authority figures and story players. It's not clear if the world here is matriarchal in the way Hurley often writes hers, but this is certainly a future of gender equality.

This is a straight-up recommendation from me: Go for the fried snake, stay for the exploration of post-war trauma and Machiavellian thinking.

Axiom's End
Lindsay Ellis
470 pages
Titan Books
Review by Andrew Chidwick

I've known about Lindsay Ellis for a while because of her excellent YouTube videos discussing films and other media, usually in a historical and/ or political context. Jumping from that to writing a science-fiction adventure seems like a big leap, but Ellis is able to adapt her analytical side, making for a riveting and topical story.

A cryptic government memo has been leaked to the public by a celebrity conspiracy theorist, a memo that hints at the US government having engaged in first contact with extra-terrestrials. Set firmly in the Bush era of 2007, *Axiom's End* opens with the leaker's daughter Cora Sabino, an early-twenties linguistics student who learns that her family is inextricably linked to the US government's cover-up of this first contact. Once she discovers how much danger she and her family are in from both aliens and the government, she finds herself becoming an interpreter for one of the aliens and a mediator between the two species. During all this her estranged father continues to attack the government with even more revelations that

threaten to destroy everything.

I was pleasantly surprised by how readable Ellis' writing style was given her academic background, and I flew through her fast-paced adventure. Cora is an immediately endearing and relatable character who goes through every kind of emotional hell, starting with the selfishness of her estranged father and continuing on through almost every character who claims to know what's best for both species. Her only solace comes from the company of a character who can't understand human emotions, out of which comes a complex but beautiful friendship that is never entirely comfortable.

This book is written with a US reader chiefly in mind, so I found a lot of the government jargon quite hard to follow at times. Some of that is deliberate - the CIA, along with the US government in general, are portrayed as shifty and unknowable - but the only times I felt lost were in the midst of agencies and departments that I barely understood.

The themes come into much sharper focus through Cora's job as an interpreter for the aliens. The phrase 'truth is a human right' comes up constantly, but Cora is also shown to paraphrase what the aliens are saying to the American authorities, contrasting sharply with how her father, through his WikiLeaks-style website, uses facts for his personal gain. Cora faces a lot of difficult choices in the story, but it's when these choices directly relate to language and truth that it really shines.

Ellis has packed a lot of politically charged ideas into her sci-fi romp, but it's not just the government she is criticising but all people who act in bad faith, even when the survival of two species is on the line. Despite the brief moments where I became lost in American government/alien/noughties jargon, seeing these horrible people through Cora's eyes kept the stakes believable and Cora herself sympathetic. Cora was a brilliantly crafted character, and her journey was a delight to follow. Any fan of a fast-paced adventure will definitely be in for a treat.

I think I understand why Lindsay Ellis set her novel in 2007 instead of the present. No-one knows how the Trump Administration would react to the arrival of aliens, but by setting it in the noughties it becomes an actual political thriller where there is at least some doubt as to whether the US government will do the worst possible thing. The Bush Administration was nonetheless rife with mistrust, greed and criminality, allowing Ellis to create a fresh and cynical take on first contact.

Ed Bentley's wife has left him and he's been dropped by his publisher. Still, it's not the end of the world. All he has to do is ghost-write a science-fiction novel for Tuppy Cotton, a YouTuber young enough to be his daughter…

When Ed uncovers an unearthly mystery at Tuppy's Yorkshire retreat, everything changes. The world might not be ending, but it will be turned upside down.

Ace Doubles is Eric Brown's dazzling and moving tribute to his heroes: the writers who captured his imagination in his youth, inspiring him to become an award-winning author; and the ordinary people who do extraordinary things.

Published by Stone Owl Stories, an imprint of Shoreline of Infinity

Stone Owl Series editor: Andrew J. Wilson

Ace Doubles

Eric Brown

118pp

paperback and digital formats

www.shorelineofInfinity.com

Shoreline of Infinity is based in Edinburgh, Scotland, and began life in 2015.

Shoreline of Infinity Science Fiction Magazine is a digital magazine published monthly in PDF, ePub and Kindle formats. It features new short stories, poetry, art, reviews and articles.

We are open for submissions from new and established writers – details of our regular submission windows are available on our website.

But there's more – we run regular live science fiction events called Event Horizon, with a whole mix of science fiction related entertainments such as story and poetry readings, author talks, music, drama, short films – we've even had sword fighting. Event Horizon is mostly monthly, and before covid-19 we hosted them live, in a real venue, with people mingling – hard to imagine, eh? We're online now, of course, but that does mean you can join in from anywhere in the world.

When we return to venue events, we will continue to livestream them, though. For details, visit the website.

We also publish a range of science fiction linked books, take a look at our collection at the Shoreline Shop. You can also pick up back copies of all of our issues, thanks to the wonders of digital publishing and print on demand. Details on our website

www.shorelineofinfinity.com

A Science Fiction Ghost Story

Flash fiction competition for Shoreline of Infinity Readers

At Christmas, everyone enjoys the thrill of a ghost story. This year, we want a science fictional ghostly tale to scare the bejeesus out of us. You have 1,000 words, starting *now*.

Prizes

£50 for the winning story, plus 1-year digital subscription to *Shoreline of Infinity*. Two runners-up will each receive a 1-year digital subscription to Shoreline of Infinity.

The top three stories will be published in the December issue *Shoreline of Infinity* – all three finalists will receive a print copy of this edition.

The detail

Maximum 1,000 words, one story per submitter.

The story must not have been previously published.

Deadline for entries: midnight (UK time) 5th September 2021.

To enter, visit the website at:

www.shorelineofinfinity.com/2021ffc

There's no entry fee, but on the submission entry form you will be asked for a certain word from this issue 23 of Shoreline of Infinity, so have this ready by your side.

Also available from

www.shorelineofInfinity.com

Cover artwork - Union by Alex Storer
https://thelightdreams.wordpress.com